The Man Who Fell in Love

Jon Persico

I0460346

Printfields Ltd, London

FOR LOVE

You have led me here.
A world I am not prepared for.
And yet craved all my life.

J. Persico

I

TWO WORDS

Love.
Love is one word.
But your heart contains two.
Can two words mean more than anything else in the world? More than love itself?

This story begins with a dance.
A Sacred Dance.
Israel. A place of love and sacrifice.
In a kibbutz, where everything is recycled. Even your soul.

With my mind and my body in chaos, I have arrived to a retreat, a sacred dance meditation. My chaos has a need, a wish, a notion, and an idea.

A need to cleanse the mind from a mountain of words and discord of voices. I want to hear my heart and soul again.

A wish to break my body free from the many prisons of my own limitations. My body was never taught to dance. And a body has a way of remembering what it was never taught.

A notion that to pause will allow my being to heal. But what will happen after the healing?

An idea that by cleaning, breaking and pausing, I will face my truth, stare at my 'self' and maybe even see my soul for the first time.

But why am I here?

Yes, I am scared.

Terrified? No.

I am hurting.

I feel emptiness. I just do not know where it is. It has consumed me completely.

And there is a problem.

I have never looked inside.

I have no reflection.

I have never seen myself.

Just like the Camino de Santiago, an endless journey that finds you, even if you cannot find yourself, this beautiful land to which I have some mysterious connection has found me once more and brought me.

And just like the Camino de Santiago, with my first steps of the sacred dance my mind learns to leave the chaos behind. And with the next steps, the next dance, I enter a space where a new story is being written around me.

And stories lead to unexpected worlds.

This story is about the discovery of a spectacular feeling buried away by a world unable to cope with spectacular feelings.

Jerusalem in October.

The rains have yet to mark the coming of the olive harvest.

But you came.

You came to Jerusalem.

After five days of dancing together in the kibbutz with fifty other broken souls through broken silences, broken meals and broken evenings, we parted. I travelled east, to Jerusalem, and you headed west, to the sea.

And when the sixth day fell, unbroken by the new sunrise, you followed the freshly painted yellow arrows in the air to Jerusalem. To find me.

I remember the moment you discovered me. I remember stepping towards you.

You were standing alone. I can still see what you were wearing. But most of all, I remember your eyes, the way you looked at me, the way you looked directly into my eyes. I smiled, you smiled.

I remember the light around you, the air, the buildings framing the moment. Framing your presence. The yellow arrows were pointing to the two of us in that moment.

A moment of magic.

An unexpected moment.

We were hungry, we walked to the restaurant and ordered orange soup, but the waiter apologised for it was late and the restaurant pot was empty.

Instead, we returned home and filled the pot with passion, we made love.

How do you write about love? How do you write about making love?

Two lovers sitting on a bed fully clothed.

'What shall we do?' I ask.

'I don't know,' you laugh.

We sit on the cusp of a crevice. Ready to fall.

Not afraid of the leap.

Not afraid of making love.

Not afraid of flying.

Only afraid of falling.

And having never stood on the edge before.

Having never seen the earth below, or the condition of our lives that wait in the aftermath below, we sit on the edge, afraid of broken bones, terrified of broken hearts.

How does a lover write about love?

The first touch.

The sensation under the finger tips.

The softness of the skin.

The scent of a need, a desire, a healing.

The kiss.

The kiss.
The lips on the skin.
And a body that aches with a language of words that only the other can read.

A body that speaks.
A body that screams.
A face that smiles.
A face that remembers love once forgotten.
A face that shines.

Tear away all the notions of love.
Rip away all the ideas of love.
Wash away all the sermons on love wrapped inside the sins of churches, the rules of temples, the sermons of synagogues and the callings of the mosques.
Remove all the wrappings, flavourings and colourings from the meanings of the word love.
And what is left?
Something pure.
Something raw.
Something simple.

A feeling.

Not a word, a feeling.

A moment that carries you into another life. One that you might have wished to have lived earlier but in fact, were never ready for.

A moment that reaches into the abyss and touches the essence of life, sees the divine light for the first time, and screams with bliss to the universe.

A flame that only reaches and burns after the abstinence, the loneliness, the solitude, the hurt, the rejection, the loss of being, the soul that had to die in the chaos of emptiness in order to feel the glory of the waiting passion.

And what glory.

A shared passion, need, desire, that creates such energy and pleasure that it reaches the top of a mountain.

And the sensation on the peak is one.

A oneness with which you let go, leap into the heaven above and fly.

You feel the new life force, the life energy stretching your body into the earth and into the sky and so you raise your hand, you stretch your fingers and you know you are touching the divine.

Your body was made for this moment of bliss.

You know it is holy.

Your heart was always beating for this ultimate ache.

And when you arrive, a door invites you into a new universe.

The door surprises you. You had never seen it before.

It was hidden. Where had it been all this time?

Hidden by the world.

Invisible.

Or maybe love was invisible.

Maybe you were invisible.

Maybe your heart was invisible.

But the door was always there.

You open the door.

And for the first time in your life you say two words, two words to your lover with a genuine heart, a heart that has learned to forgive.

Two words that mean more than anything else in your world, more than love itself.

More than life.

And you close your eyes.

II

JERUSALEM

A brilliant full moon hangs outside the window, watching.

An embrace is waiting inside the room.

Will the shadows of the moonlight remember our waiting souls?

'What shall we do?' I ask.

'I don't know,' you laugh.

I don't want to remember who said it first, but I am glad it was you. 'Let's keep the underwear on.'

I remember your voice, confident, reassuring. It's ok.

I am terrified deep inside.

Can I make love?

Can anyone love me?

Can anyone want to make love with me?

The journey from one bed, an empty bed, into another where love is waiting.

I need to tell her that lovemaking is new for my body. My mind is scared. Full of fears.

But I say nothing.

I hold her.

The sensation of holding a woman is a dream, a deep desire lain inside my soul, dormant for years. A heart that has been waiting. How long? 20 years? 30 years? All my life? It does not matter.

A heart that has forgiven the wait. But a heart still waiting.

For me? Right now, in this place, on this bed? Just holding her is enough.

I should tell her.

I say nothing.

Instead, I let the silence speak. Something about her. Something about this moment guides and takes us. I wrap her in my arms, I feel her on my skin. My fingertips stretch to feel and touch her. I am looking for her soul.

I sense her. Her need. Her desire. Or is it my need, my desire I am imagining?

I feel her. I know it is her voice. The softness, the calm, and my breathing slows.

I close my eyes and allow my senses to see her.

She is comfortable in my arms. As if my arms have always been waiting for her.

There is nothing more to think or do.

Just hold her. It is enough.

She makes it easy.

Her body moves to caress me.

Her warmth makes me warm.

Her softness, her sense, her being speaks to my being, my presence.

I can make love to her, she says, and yet no words are spoken.

She feels.

She makes it easy for me to feel.

My fingers caress her senses. They reach her neck, followed by the lips.

The lips reach her breasts and the fingers struggle with the bra straps and the bra falls to her legs. So do the fingers.

I do not remember when the lovemaking began.

But time had no meaning in that moment.

The universe stopped.

An endless moment.

It took us both to another world that we had never explored.

A wondrous place.

How does a lover describe the places that love visits?

I have crossed deserts to see giant monsters.

Swam through canyons.

Jumped into gorges.

Climbed to the top of mountains.

I have walked across countries, skied down mountains, dived with sharks and jellyfish.

I have travelled to far off lands with great walls, floated in the lowest ocean, and touched the highest glaciers. I have tracked the last desert leopard and waved at the palace of the ancient Queen of Sheba.

But nothing can prepare you for the new land you are about to step into, where the voices are only spoken with the eyes. Where the language can only be touched by the hands and fingers, and where the grammar, the vocabulary, is as simple as gentleness, or is it the tenderness, of the kiss? Grammar is always confusing.

And nothing, no-one has ever told you about the simplicity and beauty of the sharing of the feeling we call love.

That is because no being, no one, can ever describe love, there is no language called love, no dictionary of love.

The subject of love has been lost, maybe even erased from memory of the living, only the word remains, but the soul cannot discard the memory of a world of feelings, a world of love for which life was created.

A soul waiting to be shared, has now touched and tasted the words of a prayer.

So this is faith.

And love is beyond any dogma and religion.

No one can tell you what love is, it is already inside you - just like happiness and joy - just waiting to be released and waiting to shine. Waiting to give life to your body and soul.

In that moment, in Jerusalem, you woke my soul and my body, they had not just been waiting, they had been sleeping, dormant. In fact, till that moment, the soul and the body had been dreaming and living in a fantastical world. A fantasy world.

And now I am being loved.

I can feel love.

I can sense love.

I hold her as if I will never hold a woman again.

I know she feels my emptiness, my fear, the heaviness inside.

Somehow, she understands.

She senses my fragile freshly waking soul. She touches it with hers.

She shares with me her soul, allowing my soul to break through the mind of shields that had protected it from pain, and she brings to me a taste of the passion and joy of her soul.

We make love.

Minutes become hours. Our bodies did more than wake each other.

And then I see her tears.

Wet eyes. Beautiful wet eyes. Tears hiding a joy.

But I have never seen such tears before.

'Am I hurting you?' I ask. 'Shall I stop?'

'No,' you say. 'Carry on. I have been waiting for this moment all my life.'

I did not understand those words.

But I do understand this feeling of laying next to the most beautiful woman in the world.

I close my eyes and open them, she is still there. She is sleeping next to me. I do not want to sleep. I just want to stare at her. Her hair, her skin. Her gentleness. I am laying next to her softness.

I wake in the early morning. In a few hours I will be leaving, making my way to the airport.

I open my eyes and see her next to me. The dream is real. She is real. I kiss her neck just below her ears.

I kiss her again. She stirs.

I hold her.

We wake up making love.

For now, the only light is the divine light of the orange moon over Jerusalem.

III

A NEW LAND

We have known each other for several weeks, been lovers for two nights, messages and calls have filled the gaps since our previous parting, and a spontaneous decision brings us together once more which feels like an unexpected, random, embrace.

But in life, nothing is spontaneous, and in love, nothing is random.

Like everyone, we both have a need, a need for love, a hope to explore another good heart. Something special happened to our bodies in Jerusalem, and that sensation of joy and happiness has touched our souls.

Neither of our hearts can let the feeling go.

The body knows what is right. It craves the right, the healing, the touch, to be held. And now, the body has felt the touch.

The soul knows what is good. The soul seeks goodness. To be nourished, it only knows goodness. And now it has touched goodness.

Only the mind is confused, busy analysing every decision, every moment, finding reasons, explanations and pretending to know the heart and the soul, but it is only a bridge between the heart and soul.

Her mind is unsure. I am unsure.
A risk. A gamble. We both know.
Our relationship may work, it may not. We both accept. But we want to try. We want to see.

The bridge between our hearts has already crossed a sea. We have both already felt the connection and recognise the sensations, the caress of two souls.

When I arrive at the airport, you welcome me with a beautiful embrace.

When my arms reach around you, you do not see, but my eyes close and begin to water.

I am holding joy.

And I have never held such softness before.

Your embrace does not immediately confess, but in the car we both confess.

You are nervous too.

Over the next days I will be introduced to three cats, two dogs and delightful nineteen year old twins, a boy and a girl, who breeze in and out of your life at weekends.

But first I am introduced to the bedroom.

I cannot help but notice the books.

The ones that immediately capture my interest sit flat on the far left on the bookshelf above the bed. They appear discarded.

"The land of O."

And, as if the subject still needs elaboration, one more book lays on top of the first.

"The Peak of Lovemaking."

And finally, regal, upon the throne of both elaborations, proudly sits a very satisfied teddy bear.

The titles intrigue.

It is late, and the journey was long. So I shower. I am naked, I am already in bed. As I watch you enter the room, I begin to learn your insecurities. Over the next days we will learn much about each other. For now, I see you always like to keep something on.

I undress you, we hold each other. A precious moment that slowly steps into the intimate passion of the dance of lovers. A dance that will be repeated the following days and nights.

Even if each time we embrace, we attempt to relive and recreate the moment in Jerusalem, we find ourselves moving with new choreography in every new moment, exploring longer, touching something deeper, exploring new lands.

And then, one evening, you tell me the meaning of those words you said in Jerusalem, 'I have been waiting for this moment all my life.'

You tell me that that you are experiencing something special. Your first moment of bliss, the first in your life, was with me, during our first nights together. That moment when you wept as we made love. That moment your eyes were filled with tears. Wet eyes that have painted the memory forever. The moment is now inside me. Shared with me forever. A part of me, forever.

What did you see in that moment of bliss?

Was the vision what you expected?

What did you find inside that moment?

Did you recognise yourself?

Did you know yourself?

Maybe it was not a vision at all, but a feeling. What did you feel?

And how have you lived these years without that feeling, that moment?

How does the body, with this new life inside, feel now?

And then you tell me that the exploration is not finished. You are still experiencing new sensational sensations.

Our lovemaking is guiding you to new lands and new mountains. Endless moments of bliss. Mountains that take you higher, above the clouds, a palace filled with sensations lasting longer and longer.

How long does it last? I asked in wonderment.

Forever, you said.

We were both becoming explorers.

Your previous partners must have been far more experienced than I, and so I still do not understand.

Why did that moment wait for me before it arrived to you? What part do I play in this dance? What am I doing that is different? What is my purpose? Do I have a purpose?

You tried to explain. You said my touch was different. It was heaven. The way I held you was different. Like being in heaven.

I still do not understand. Does not every man hold their lover the same way, as if they are holding their entire existence in their arms? Does not everyone touch a lover that precious way, the only way to touch this gorgeous, irreplaceable, fragile, unexplainable feeling of love between you? Is not every lover's touch the same? A touch that has always been a dream? How else do you touch a lover, a dream?

But there are no answers, only more mysteries.

And if I do not understand, I try to believe that it is not just a touch, not just a way of holding, it is the feeling deep inside me.

When I hold you, the sensation in my fingers and on my skin reaches my eyes. I have a feeling in my eyes that make my eyes close while I explore every sensation of you. I have a feeling in my ears when I hear you breathe, when I hear your voice. I have a feeling in my lips when I kiss you, your neck, your shoulder, everywhere I kiss you, my lips feel different, as if they are talking with your body. I have a feeling in my skin where my skin touches yours. I have a feeling in my mind when it surrenders to you, and I sense my soul touches yours as we create that small universe around us where only you and I exist.

Is this why you feel different when I touch you? When I hold you?

And in that moment of holding you, you and I are all that matter. The universe has touched our souls and knows that too. For the universe has created us for nothing other than to love.

For without love, the universe can never know life.

And if the universe has been waiting too, it is for nothing other than every moment of love on earth.

IV

THE DAWN

The past and the now.

A relationship from the past that allows me to feel the now.

A past that I lived for too long.

My body died in that relationship. A union of companionship and caring, yes, but also filled with naivety. Two people sharing the same house, the same bed, without the touch that heals, without the embrace of lovers. A relationship that did not know the recipe for loving, only living.

My skin died first.

A skin that craved the touch. The touch of healing. The touch of life.

My body died after. A body that craved the embrace of a lover, to leave behind the universe of lost souls.

I thought and believed, all those years, that my relationship was normal. That things would change.

My soul sobbed when, after the walk through the denial, I realised I had become an empty vessel. My mind wept knowing that I had never felt the passion of desire in my arms and believed that I would never enter that universe of feeling.

I do not blame my partner, only myself. I let my body die.

It was my choice to remain in that relationship.

But, since my attractive partner did not desire me, I also came to the conclusion that no one else would or could. I resigned myself to believing that I was not capable of knowing love and passion, would never know what it was to hold a lover, to make love, to know the feelings that heals bodies and completes souls.

My mistakes, my stupidity, my naivety.

Twilights and dawns.

You have woken me.

Now that I know your journey to bliss, you have led me into a special place. Another new feeling, a new belief. Something I could not have seen or known before. That when I make love with you, I can unlock the door of new pleasure, a new heaven for you. A door that opens to a new spectacular world for you to explore, feel and experience an ultimate joy. I had no idea anything like this was possible between lovers. That I could lead you to any door.

Is this what our bodies and souls can do for one another?

And now that I am stepping through the door with you too, the freshness of this new world overwhelms me. Until you, I did not even know I could make love. Feel love. Know love. Know the doors to love.

Know the doors to souls.

You describe your fears of the past. How those old fears have dissolved away. You describe how our lovemaking touches you somewhere new, somewhere you have not been before, felt before. Somewhere deep inside your body and it touches you again and again, and it takes you to the sky, to heaven. You said the fear of the past had now become a hunger. A longing, a need to be touched again and again.

You said our love and our lovemaking was washing your body.

I love those words. Your words, not mine.

I never ever imagined that phrase.

What a beautiful meaning the combination of those words creates.

And after I sensed the meaning, I sensed the cleansing.

When you said I looked different, my face, is different. I could not imagine.

But as I absorb those words, I see that you look and feel softer, younger, healthier, and when I tell you, you are not surprised.

Now, when you tell me that my face is different when I hold you, I realise you are seeing me in the other world.

And in that world, my eyes see you in a different light. You are much more than a touch.

Because you have a different light.

I never thought, or knew, that feeling the sensations of love and lovemaking feeds our souls, and take us to our souls.

I can feel your light.

You helped me understand that our love was different, you used the word 'innocent', and the freshness of our feelings was generating a very powerful life force. A force that evicts insecurities, regenerates the body, removes the dust and the layers of the past, leaving behind an essence of life, and a soul that breathes a new nectar of fresh existence.

Our bodies have been created for this. This moment, this feeling.

Being with you completes me so many ways.

The way you see the world. The places where you take me.

Now I can give words to this new feeling
and sensation that is filling me,
completing me, I am feeling my soul and
the life, the energy you describe, inside me
for the first time. In fact, I knew this
feeling when I held you for the first time, I
just never knew how to spell the words.

And when I hold you, and when I feel
you, and when you see me in that other
world, I wonder how you feel, I wonder
where you are?

I would like to believe there is a
connection.

I will never know your land of O and
you will never know mine. But our
moments together, the moments we share,
bring together our bodies, our souls, our
minds, our hearts. We create a connection
that speaks to the universe in gratitude.

Or maybe it is the universe that looks
upon us and smiles with gratitude.

The only thing I am sure of is that
when I am close to you, with you, when I
touch you, hold you, make love with you, I

have not felt this prayer before. A prayer that has been granted.

When we are making love, when I am holding you, I sense you, the body under your skin, your heart. I sense your soul, and I feel your body shiver. I taste electricity inside you. I feel so complete, so at one with you in my arms. Like my body and soul have been waiting for you. That moment of holding each other is much more than the embrace. We are inside each other's bodies, souls, fulfilling a moment that has been waiting a lifetime. A moment that lasts a lifetime. For now I know, every time we are together, we are living so many lives.

When my body holds you, and when my lips kiss you. An endless ecstasy washes me, fills me, bathes me, completes me. I too feel an endless pleasure. I too feel the utmost magic.

And if this is the force of life, how have I lived without life all these years, all this time?

A cloud of sadness momentarily envelopes my mind when I remember. Now I know why I felt so empty, so lost. And

the melancholy lifts quickly too. I only
have to turn my head and look at you,
touch you, you are real. I see you in your
eyes and the memory of the past lifts
away.

I am feeling for the first time in my life.
I am feeling.
I am feeling your light.
There is no before.
Before the now. Before the light.
More than light has touched my skin,
entered my heart.
You have entered.
The body that had died is beating with
a new heart.
I no longer see the colour of the light
that was the before.
Before you.
Each new morning's waking takes away
more of the darkness.
The sunrise lifts away the before, and
brings the curiosity of the now and the
presence of the after.
Each new morning, I wake, I look out of
the window, I turn and see you.

If you have woken, I see your eyes looking at me.

The sun shines into your eyes.

The light that surrounds you is the new sunrise.

Each new day has become enchanted, extraordinary, magical even, because I am waking up with you next to me. That moment and the memory of that moment's waking becomes a lifetime.

Each morning I wake with the sunlight and I turn to look at you. You are usually facing away from me, I gaze at your back, your skin, your neck, your hair, to feel so much without touching is the love I feel and the joy of love I feel every morning when I open my eyes. I cannot hear you breathing, but I know you are real, you are here, and every morning, when I wake, you are the most beautiful woman in the world. The most beautiful woman I will ever wake up with in my life. I want to kiss you. I want to wake you. I want you to feel my soul, my body, my desire.

But you have already warned me that you are a bear in the mornings. A wild angry bear if woken too early. I laugh at the thought because I am not sure I believe you. In Jerusalem I woke you at three in the morning and we made love.

But this is a different space.

Your space.

Your bed.

Your home.

Your life I am invading.

So instead, I stay awake and look at you. Look at every beautiful millimetre of you, and fill my eyes with your beauty. Your nearness.

I am waking with you next to me. My existence in this moment is a complete lifetime.

And every morning I wake in this bed, when I open my eyes I see the dawn light and see you next to me, I live a new lifetime.

I have lived and loved those moments, those dawns, those lifetimes, over and over again with you, every morning.

You do not know.

Your eyes were closed.

You were sleeping.

You were dreaming.

You will never know.

V

THE FIRST TIME

The first time I met you.

I sat with you. I looked into your eyes and you looked into mine.

You asked me a question.

"Who is inside you?"

Words with a mysterious and magic power.

Was the magic in the sound of each of those words?

Or maybe the mystery was in your voice.

My eyes responded first. I cried. For I could not bear to look inside me.

I could not bear to feel the emptiness inside.

But even empty wounds need to bleed.

Your words drew a pause in my body, the pause allowed the words, like a key, to find the lock and free the emptiness, and the emptiness bled pain.

Painful tears from a long lost and deep, hoped-to-be-forgotten place.

But despair is never forgotten.

Memories and scars are always present.

My eyes weep even now when I touch the memory of that place.

Your voice that held me. Kept me from falling.

Your voice held me, gripped me, calmed me.

After the calm, the words came with the tears.

And you listened to my heart.

And in that moment you looked into my eyes, you looked through my broken tears, my broken heart and to the love that cascades through every space and every moment in my soul.

There, I felt you.

I felt you looking at me, searching for me.

I felt as if I was touching the echo of your soul.

When my words no longer flowed. Your echo led me to the now. I raised my face and I followed the echo into your eyes.

And your eyes led me inside of you.

There, I saw small reflections of my soul, my being, my existence.

You were looking at me.

And after seeing these reflections of me, being seen, I wept even more.

I cried so much. You only saw some of the tears.

I wept inside.

For you saw me.

I acknowledged that you could see me when I could not, and in that moment I loved your eyes, I loved your soul. I loved your presence.

There, in that moment, my journey to the feelings of love began.

For in that moment your soul loved me.

We hugged afterwards.

I do not remember the feel of the embrace.

But I do remember the pain that had been drawn to the surface and was enveloping me.

All I could feel was the weeping of a heart and soul that only wants to love, and hold the love of a lover.

I felt as if the pain and the weeping would never stop.

I remember my face being wet.

I did not wipe the tears. I wanted the skin on my face to feel the bite of every tear, to remember the depth from where they had emerged.

The sharp teeth of those tears now feel like bites from another world. A world once filled with big important words like money, car, possessions, shopping trips, outings and holidays.

A world where one small word was missing.

And without that small word.

My heart was empty.

My whole world felt empty. A void that possessions could not fill.

A world where I could not feel.

And that was the problem.

I had stopped feeling.

And now, I am inside a new world.
You have led me here.
A world I have not prepared for.
And yet craved all my life.

And in this new world, I am holding
heaven in my arms.
And these new tears, are feeling the
bite of joy, the love inside me is free. Free
to love.
You set me free.
You set my love free.
Not just the word, but my soul.

I am dancing, moving, feeling, crying,
relaxing, sensing the world, filling the void
and learning to love.

I cup my hands and let my body and
my heart fill with your love, every time you
look at me, every time you show me love.
Every time you want to love me, I leap.
I find each moment of your giving, a
moving, divine experience, a devotion.

I have to pause, each time, to submerge myself in the feeling. To feel you.

But the pause also carries something else unexpected.

A surprise. A fear.

I am scared.

I realise I am also scared of this new love.

I cannot understand why.

Am I scared of accepting love? Am I asking if I deserve so much joy?

Is it possible that accepting your love, accepting that I am worthy of your love, is harder than showering you with my love?

I asked many more questions.

I came to a conclusion.

I do not know how to accept love.

No one has ever loved me the way you do.

As days passed, as I lingered in that moment of pause and felt the fear, the uncertainty, I explored the fear and the uncertainty.

And when I came to understand and accept the feeling, to know the fear. I realised it was not fear after all.

There was no barrier to accepting love.

It was simply a reaction that made me pause. A reaction to an unknown.

The depth of love you offer me is so unknown to me.

The depth of love I feel inside is so unknown to me.

The feelings are overflowing.

My reaction is to pause.

I am experiencing surprise.

I am overwhelmed.

I am glad I was overwhelmed.

Just like I was overwhelmed when I saw a Van Gogh or a Monet for the first time.

I could have just breezed through rooms of the gallery and strolled as I might along a street just admiring my surroundings. But when I stopped and let the surprise of the painting take me, it left me breathless.

And when I paused in front of the painting, my breath, my eyes entered the world of the brush strokes.

My mind scattered into each brush stroke trying to see the moment captured by each and every bristle in this new world in front of me. Even my body sensed the new as I stepped deeper inside the vision created in front of me.

So when you love me, I am pausing.

Every time you smile at me, touch me, move towards me, I am pausing every time.

First it is surprise.

And when I realise how amazing and gorgeous that moment is, I just need to pause and allow the feelings that I am sensing to rain all over me.

There are no umbrellas.

I want to absorb every drop, become saturated, float and swim inside the feelings.

Accepting love was not the fear. But the new sensations they drew were overwhelming.

When I felt the flutter in my stomach, when I calmed and I stopped and looked, I saw a new moment full of butterflies.

Butterflies that led me to the freshness of your touch.

Butterflies that led me to the consequence of your smile.

The love you are giving comes from your soul, body and mind. And it is for me.

Imagine how that feels.

Yes, I am overwhelmed.

I want to pause forever.

I never want to walk past.

I want to love everything inside that pause.

I want to stand, I want to feel, welcome the feelings, and love the feelings back to you.

The greatest gift I have ever received.

Let me feel the shiver through my body and my mind.

Let me sense and accept the mystery and magic of how this is happening and feel my soul floating.

Let me absorb your love slowly, be
patient with me as I drink every drop.
Let me feel. I want to feel.
My life has never felt this love before.
I want to be here forever.
Surrounded by butterflies.

I see our painting.
You and I are in an intimate embrace.
I see the wings on both of us.
Yes, we are in heaven.

I love this world, this new heaven.
But in this new world I have to learn a
new language.
I have never been good with languages.
Now I sense and feel new words, but I
do not yet know what the words are.

Extraordinary.
The feeling is extraordinary.

Is there no end to the joy, to the
pleasure of love?
To the bliss of making love?

Is it possible that this feeling, this pleasure, gets stronger and stronger everyday?

For every day, our love, when we see each other, our lovemaking when we feel each other, is taking us to new and intense worlds.

The love you are giving me, is everything I have dreamed of.

In Jerusalem you said you had been waiting for that moment all your life.

Now I, at last, understand.

I have been waiting for this moment all my life too.

VI

FLAWS AND FEARS

When we love, the cages, prisons and walls around our hearts, bodies and souls crumble and begin to fall away.

Cages of denial.

Prisons full of limits. Prisons to protect us from pain. And prisons, ironically, full of pain.

Walls and barriers to ourselves and to love. Walls of emptiness, scared to love. Bleak walls, unadorned with memories.

Now, after the eruption of love, a mountain of rubble remains.

Our lover sweeps away the rubble.

Our love takes away the scattered pieces.

Our love, our touch, our embrace, our lovemaking, what we see in each other's eyes, our new feelings, begin to replace the rubble, with life.

A life we only dreamed of.

Love has exposed our desires.

To a mind that once refused to see.

We bare ourselves.

We uncover our souls.

But souls also have their own secrets, hidden away.

Shadows inside the rubble.

Still dark when uncovered. Still caged, still imprisoned.

Love uncovers new shadows, our scars and flaws.

Past lives.

Past fears.

Past love.

Past hurt.

Past wounds.

Even past monsters.

The love, the scars, the flaws, makes us who we are. Make us feel love the way we do.

And the woman in front of me, my lover, is discovering my flaws, my scars, and yet she loves me as I am, with all my flaws and fears.

The thought of her love is powerful and brings me to the essence of the creator inside her. I adore her.

And no one else has loved me with my flaws and fears before.

Love is precious.

And being loved with the flaws and the scars and monsters, is being loved without expectations. The most precious love between lovers.

I feel my lover in my body every time I look at her.

I want her as she is.

With her flaws.

With her scars.

With her monsters.

I adore her as she is.

With her flaws.

With her scars.

With her monsters.

I love her. All of her.

But while loving her, making love with her, while the moment washes away another mountain of rubble. Vulnerable shadows are exposed.

Hurt buried deep inside.

Past hurt.

The monster roars to the surface, wanting to be set free.

And I too, want to be free of the monster.

The scars, and the pain is me. The past me. The monster is me.

My monster surfaced when you uttered three words.

My instinct was to fight. Deny the monster. I did not use the moment to unlock the chain and set the monster free.

The monster was not the problem, my response to the monster was the flaw.

You saw my reaction, my flinch, to your words,

'I love you,' you said.

We were in bed.

Three words.

And in that moment, those three words carried me away into a past world, a past relationship of "I love you"s. A world where I did not want to hear any more "I love you"s.

For in that world, 'I love you' had another meaning, another purpose. A comfort.

A comfort to a pain I did not want to feel any more.

You noticed the trigger.

You noticed my journey as I recoiled into my past.

My past pain.

It lasted a day, it lasted the night.

I hurt you. My reaction hurt you.

I caused you pain.

I know I hurt you. You wept.

But when I emerged, when I woke in the morning, I found you holding my hand.

You held me.

I did not say how vulnerable I felt.

I did not need to explain how much hurt and weight those rusted chains linked with the three words still had around me.

The trigger, and my reaction surprised me too.

I thought the meaning of those words was in the past.

Had been lost.

But I had not yet erased the pain.

And the hurt returned to my mind and my body.

And my hurt, brought tears to your eyes.

I felt lost.

Trying to avoid looking at the monster.

I could not admit that my new feelings for you were still littered by the rubble of the past.

Scared even.

Scared of the next page.

Scared of the next chapter.

Scared to accept your words.

Our words, our actions and behaviours now have a new meaning, have a new feeling, have a new weight. A weight of new love.

But shadows still litter new love.

You showed me that we need a moment to understand the newly revealed shadows, scars of despair, the marks of the past, and to bridge them by unlinking the chains of the past from the present, and absorb the weight of the meaning of our new feelings, new love, the now.

This weight in my chest? A heaviness.

I know the weight is the new unknown, an affection, feeling for you. An affection I have never felt for anyone before.

My craving, my need, my want.

To look at you every morning, night, day.

I know the weight is gratitude that I am feeling love, baring and feeling my soul, feeling, so much love for the first time in my life.

A need to feel you.

A need to be near you.

How do I unlatch, unhook, set free and release this monster from my heart, let go of my scars? Return the scars to their rightful place? How do I let the scars heal and discard the meanings of the past?

Those three words that hurt me in the past? Now, I have to learn to love each syllable again.

But the fear of that other world remains.

Why am I so scared of that other world. The world of a past life.

If the words escape me, escape my voice, will I return to the other world?

Will my new world of love disappear?

I want to set those words free.

If the words leave me now, the monster threatens me, that I will sob, I will fall apart. The words will leave behind broken pieces of me and my new life, my new love.

I am just getting to know this new me.

The new me that is loved, being loved.

What does the colour and the passion of each letter in the graffiti of love look like?

I want to feel, sense the colour of each letter, feel the softness of each of those syllables. The joy and the pain of that last

word. A word that was once empty of
passion, without colour or graffiti.

Now I feel being inside you.
Feel outside of you.
Your sweat and your tears.
Feel your soul and skin.
Feel the colour of your eyes looking at
me and I see the words I have always
wanted to see, and never thought I would
ever see.
Eyes that find their way inside of me.
Eyes that uncover the treasures of love
and passion underneath the rubble,
leaving behind a new freshness of life.
Eyes that I adore so much.
Eyes that I can wake up with every
morning until the sun sets on my heart.
And when I am away, eyes that I will
look for when I wake.

Three words.
And these three words have caused me
to flinch. To pause. To remember the past
pain. And the consequence is a
melancholy and a chaos of sadness.
Which reached into your sadness.

Your tears, shatter me again.
I am the cause of the sadness.
You tell me, "I am not ready" to accept
the three words.

But I hear the three words.
I have wanted them all my life.
And after you share them.
After I feel them.
After I see them.
I know they are inside me too.
Waiting.
Craving to be released.

You are here.
You are the now.
You are the love.
You are the passion.
You are the three words.
You are in my soul.
You are the kiss.
The tears.
I kiss those tears. Your tears.
They become my tears
And through my lips, your tears have
now entered every cell of my body.
I will always carry those tears.

And when I say the words the first time, you did not notice my release.

My liberation.

I needed to cry with you when my voice released the words for the first time.

I needed to cry and take your three words and place them into my freshly released heart, a heart that has been waiting for those three words since the first heartbeat.

How can I explain.

I have been wanting to know the meaning of those words.

A new meaning.

A meaning ringing with the sound of your voice, your ecstasy, your joy.

Your smile, so many smiles.

I love your voice. I love your smile.

Love.

A new word. I find myself singing the word.

Love.

The middle word.

Sandwiched between the I and You.

Let me cry.

Let me feel alive.
Let me love.
Let me say those words out loud.
Let me fall.
And when I fall again,
And when I need to fall again,
It's ok for me too.
Let me fall.
When I am near you.
I know.
I am living LOVE.
Between I, and You.
The chain is broken. The monster is free.

The pain of the past is sent away, and every day it is further away. One day it will be over the horizon.

Your loving me, and my loving you are all I need to see and feel.

My sunrise and sunset.

I love you.

So much.

And the next time I fall, I will fall gently into your arms.

And that's all I want to do.

VII

ROOM 623

Time to leave again.

Memories to pack.

Memories to leave behind.

I open the door to leave.

I am dressed in my travel clothes, you are still in your birthday skin.

We have spent your birthday loving, dancing, holding hands while walking through the streets and along the beach and weeping at the dance in the theatre.

I look at you, all I want to do is put my arms around you one more time.

I want to hold your smile.

Feel you. Your warmth, softness.

And yet I have been holding you and feeling you all day.

Yesterday, when I was alone, I sat wondering how this moment of leaving you would feel.

That is when I discovered you inside of me.

I was surprised.

Surprised how real you felt.

I was sensing you even though you were not there.

My arms held the comfort of holding you even though you were not in my arms.

My eyes were closed and yet, I could see your eyes.

And the sadness I imagined was quickly replaced with knowledge of the joy I would feel the next time I will look at you, hold you and see your eyes.

Holding you, has become a part of me now. A part of my existence. My life.

And in the house where we have lived, we have held each other in every room.

We have made love in every room.

Today, on your birthday, there was one more room.

One more room to leave behind. Room 623.

Room 623, where I held you today.

This morning, we were anxious about parting.

Not knowing what will happen next.

I am sure you knew.

I remember the shower. You joined me. You washed me. You held me.

And then you held me again when I came out of the shower.

Did I tell you I was nervous?

As usual, I said nothing.

But this time, you knew. I could sense you too.

You knew when you touched my skin, and I kissed yours.

We are both feeling the same.

Managing the moment inside us, separately, differently.

And yet, this moment, this act of love is perfect.

Because this moment, your touch, is still a dream. And living a dream is too perfect.

The feeling I am sensing when I touch you, and the feeling I am experiencing is the 'forever, my whole life,' feeling.

And of course, that is when I hear the voice from the deep, from the chasm of shadows inside.

"You do not deserve this moment".

A phrase I have heard in songs, read in books, seen in movies.

A phrase carried by the body, put there by my past.

A voice that has still to be carried away by the rubble.

I smile at the voice.

I recognise it as my own.

I accept that it is trying to clutch at the remnants of the remains, the rubble.

I let my mind return to the perfect woman I am holding.

She is real.

So real in my arms.

And the love I feel is real.

The voice is not real, was never real.

With you in my arms, there have been so many new feelings flowing through my body, my mind. Words I have never felt before and are now eating in my soul.

If I bring all the feelings and words together? Is this love?

And then there are so many feelings with no words.

And when I stop and sense and float inside them, I enjoy the feelings without the words.

And I am mesmerised.

Being immersed in words that do not need to be spelt.

Is this being in love?

All my senses are changing.

Even breathing leaves a new taste in my mouth.

I will not touch your body for many weeks.

When we lay in bed, I held you.

I kissed your body, your skin, with my fingertips and then my hands.

I kissed your skin, your body with my lips.

Your entire body.

I held you as if I will not hold you again.

But I know I will hold you again, so I held you with a prayer.

I want my skin to carry the memory of your skin on mine.

I want my senses to steal your scent.

I want my face and body to remember your touch.

And because I am selfish, or generous, which is it? I also want to leave a memory behind. I want to leave a trace of the sensation of our love on your skin.

Tonight, when I am on a flight, when I close my eyes, I will remember you. I will remember this touch, this kiss, this embrace, holding you. I will feel your skin and softness and flow with the magic that you are leaving inside of me, that I am carrying with me.

I want to remember the feeling of your body covering me.

How do lovers share their souls before they part?

I will fly soon.

We fly together first. We make love. Sweet love. Goodbye love.

Love that is intense, nervous, anxious.

And then I held you.

I held you with my arms, my fingertips caressed your skin, and my hearts cried.

The heart that is confused because it is still discovering the landscape of love.

The heart that is still learning the feelings and letters inside the word love.

A soul that is, every day, connecting deeper with your soul.

And it is no longer the lovemaking, it is the holding you that is the heaven, the bliss in this moment.

With my fingers that still carry a memory of stroking your hair, I open the door.

With my eyes that still remember holding and stroking your back, I look at you.

With my lips that kissed your skin starting from your neck down to your waist, I say goodbye.

My body is still feeling your softness as I look at your eyes.

A parting without expectation.

But with the feeling that adores, worships you exactly as you are.

Room 623. I am dressed in my travel clothes, you are still in your birthday skin.

I kiss you. My eyes feast on you, your smile, your naked love, your perfect goodbye.

I step towards the lift, the lift door opens. I smile at you. One last look.

You close the door of room 623.

When I sat in the cab, the feelings I carried caused my eyes to weep. It was dark. So I let them weep while I smiled with the memory of you.

You messaged me the next day and told me that you did not wait for dawn. You could not sleep.

You drove home. You did not walk to the cafe on the beach as you had said you would.

You said you could not handle the parting, so you drove home.

What made you drive home?

Fear?

Love?

Fear of love?

What did you see?

You never told me.

VIII

ALONE AGAIN

I am alone again.
We are apart.
A sea is between us.

But I do not feel alone.

I want to feel you.
I am lying alone.
I feel your presence.
But I will be sleeping alone.
I want to hold you.

I do not know if I should try and read a book.
Or write a book.
Because I know I want to make love with you.

These nights, when I fall asleep, my body remembers you.

In the night, the middle of the night, I wake.

I wake to feel my hands wrapped around you and your arms and legs wrapped around me.

To feel you and hear you cry.

I kiss your tears when you reach your divine moment.

The memory of you inside me is so strong.

I can feel you.

I sleep again, but I know I will wake up alone.

I want to feel more.

I want to touch more.

I want to understand all the feelings that are emerging inside me from that one small word, love.

I want to know what I feel with you, and will never feel without you.

I want to know why I can feel you inside me.

I remember asking you if holding a lover, the feelings of touch and lovemaking, are the same for everyone.

You were patient with me.

But love is one word, no? I replied.

You explained that what you and I feel with each other is different than anything you have felt before.

I am still trying to understand those words.

Could what we are experiencing be a dream, a psalm, a prayer?

If there is such a feeling of divine bliss inside us, between us, I want to learn more, know more.

I want to know what it really means to touch you.

Your mind, your body, your heart, your kiss, your skin, your need, your passion, your scream, your love, your feelings, your sensations.

I want to feel your touch and know, really know, the sensations that arise in me.

I want?

Want is a strong word.

Know?

Why would I want to know? Why not just feel the mystery?

Why not just accept?

But the pleasure was created in me, in you.

And my pleasure is just being discovered and felt.

Unwrapping this gift now, discovering this gift, I want to understand the connection between love and my being, love and you, myself and yourself.

How I am connecting to your soul?

I want to understand our presence, together, in the universe, to the purpose of life, to the needs of our souls, to the place where this bliss was first created.

I want to know the purpose.

Even if it is life.

To live life.

And if to love and to make love is life, then everyone should become lovers.

And live.

Of course, many thinkers, lovers, poets have asked these questions. And many say that we have the essence of god within us.

When we harm another, we harm God.

Therefore, when we love another, we love God.

They say that since we are made with the same particles that once were, and will again be, part of the universe, our love is always connected to the universe.

And so when I touch you, feel your skin, make love to you, and love you, the sensation I have, the other world I feel, the sound of the spirit of the prayer that I sing and the beautiful body, that synagogue, church, temple, mosque in which I reside, you reside, that holds and celebrates the prayer, is nothing less than the essence itself, the closest path to the divine I will ever walk, the closest I will ever feel to the purpose of life, to be a human being.

To touch, to be touched.

To love and be loved.

To feel the essence of God inside you and me.

Why do I feel this way about you?
I have loved before.
But this love, these sensations when I feel you, when you touch me, when I remember you, these feelings are not like before.
So there is a truth I must accept.
Before, I was not ready for these feelings, these sensations, these words and this love. Before I was living another life. Another purpose.

Why are the feelings and sensations of love so different with you?
With you, I feel the world. Sense the energy of life around me, in me, in you.

When did these sensations emerge?
Feelings I have never dreamt, felt before, or even imagined.
Wished maybe.
But never known.

Was it a moment?
Was it a touch?

When I remember, your smile is always the first memory.

And then, always, your eyes, I love the way you look at me.

After your eyes, always, I sense the touch and the way you touch me.

And I live in your silence.

I love your wordless words. The things you do not say.

And there is a wow moment. I have not told you about this wow moment before. I am embarrassed as it seems a little adolescent. You may have seen the way I look at you when you walk into the room? The air caresses me every time. Whenever you step into the room, an energy grabs and lifts me and a gate opens to a joy that flows into my body. My heart aches with the mystery, and my eyes and my body feel consumed by this new world where I feel my soul.

Is this what they call being in love?

Small words for huge feelings that cannot have words.

There is more.
There is a forever memory.

When I stepped through airport arrivals and found you waiting for me for the first time. I can still sense the moment my arms reached around you. I can feel your skin, I can feel your hair as it touched my face, I can feel my lips kissing your neck. I remember my eyes closing.

I can still feel your hand in mine as we walked to the car. I can feel the shape of your hand, the texture, how cool your fingers felt. I still have the sensation of my fingertip stroking the skin of your hand. I feel your soul every time I hold your hand. And when I hold your hand, I feel your smile even though I do not see your face.

The forever memory is so real inside my body. Many months have passed as I write this and I can still sense and feel your fingers in my hand.

Our hands spoke even though we did not. Or was it our souls?

I am not with you.

But when I remember you, I fall into you.

Into your gentleness, softness.

And inside that falling there is always a magic when I land.

Feelings I cannot describe.

Feelings of wonder.

Is the magic inside me? Inside you? Around me?

Sensations and feelings without words must be magic, no?

Or, is love magic?

Love, being in love. Do the words matter?

My body knows, my soul knows the meaning of this magic that I feel.

Being with you, and even when I am not with you, everything feels right.

In fact, I see your face, your smile, your eyes everywhere.

In the movies, on the people around me in the cafes and bars.

The sensation of your absent presence is very powerful, moving. Emotional sometimes because no one has been inside me like this before.

It is as if my soul is projecting you everywhere I look.

You are in my eyes, inside my body.

How am I feeling you?

Right now, I am alone.

Right now, I am a lover.

Right now, we are lovers.

And when I wake in the middle of the night, it is because the universe is remembering us, remembering our love, waiting for love.

For as we love, so does the universe feel and renew itself.

Even if, right now, I am alone.

IX

HEAVEN

Will the bridge across the sea that lies between us endure our many partings and our waitings?

The bridge does endure.

There were many more returns, many more partings, many more waitings.

During one visit, you said something felt different.

You dreamt of thieves the night before I arrived.

The dream left an impression of uncertainty in you.

'I was coming to invade your space,' you said.

But the night I arrived, the thieves left empty handed.

I had only travelled with a small rucksack.

We spent the night unpacking our love.

It was a 40L rucksack.

It seemed as if the thieves did not recognise the value of the contents.

We spend a whole day in bed as we always do on the first day.

A whole day of lovemaking.

Endless moments. How many?

A day of desire.

'Again?' You teased.

I was not counting, just a need to be holding, touching, feeling you. Sensations that can only be felt with you.

I remember one morning, we just held each other.

An endless embrace. Neither of us wanted to let go.

I remember my lips on your skin as we held each other in the morning light.

My lips stayed on your lips.

Another forever moment.

A forever kiss.

How many ways did we say I love you?

The next time, it was you who came
across the sea.

This time, I waited to welcome you.

Having flown to you, seen your life,
melted into your life, felt you in your
world, you came to feel me in mine.

Of course, I was nervous.

You were entering my world, my home,
for the first time.

I wanted you to feel happy in my world.

I cleaned my home for two days.

You arrived when I was healing from a
surgery.

When I turned and saw you walk
towards me, I smiled more broadly than
the sea you had just flown over. And when
I felt your touch and we hugged, I wept
like a lost and found little child.

Feeling you, everything felt surprisingly
different from the last embrace. The
touch, the hug, your scent, your hair, your
skin.

I had no idea that the dictionary, or is
it the thesaurus of love, changes with
time.

Feelings and words changing over and over.

How can a word remain the same and the world, the world of feelings and sensations change so much and so many times?

Time changes.

But maybe love does not know time.

Is there no end to the magic hidden inside each letter of this one small word?

Love.

A word the same size as 'life'.

How can we know something we have never touched.

Only felt.

Just like life.

I am learning how it feels for a dream to come true.

You have come to me, to my home.

To my world.

To feel me in my world.

Just as you came to me in Jerusalem.

I am baring my home, my life to you.

I have an insecurity.

I feel insecure.

But then I see you snuggled in the lounge, covered by a blanket, you smile.

I see your face.

I read your smile.

I feel your smile.

Your joy.

Your contentment.

And then you say,

'I could be happy here. I am in heaven.'

Your words take me to heaven too.

I lay opposite you.

My soul lays naked before you.

My sickness.

My dirt.

My imperfections.

My ugliness.

My truth.

My past.

My heart.

My life.

And my tears.

Love tears.

Do I really deserve so much heaven?

You are so real in this heaven.
Loving you is so real.
We spend our days just holding each other.
I am touching you. Holding your hand.
Kissing you is so so real.

Is being in love the first time always like this? Full of doubts, fear that the moment is a dream, another fantasy?

The truth is I have never made love in my home before.
The rooms have never seen love before.
That touching and kissing. That feeling, is not only new to me, it is new for this home too, for every room, for every piece of furniture.
We make love in every room, on every piece of furniture.

I stroke your smile.
Your softness.
Your skin.
Your hair.
Your eyes.
Your love.

In my home.
My home is now my heaven.

On my birthday you place a small candle on an ice cream cake. When I blew the flame, it seemed like I blew away the before, and welcomed in a new life.

A new day.

I loved that day.

I loved that evening.

I have loved every day with you.

I do not know what it means to fall in love.

I only know how it feels.

Did I fall in love with you when we sat inside the church and we both cried when we heard the music? It was funny. We turned away from each other. We were each embarrassed by our tears. We laughed with each other at the steps of the church when we confessed our tears.

That day, and every day I see you, I have the same feelings.

I fall in love with you every day.

Soon you will leave.

And when you leave, the real will instantly become the absent.

The absent will fill the spaces and the silence. The shadow of your presence will fill the memory of the house and my soul when I step into the rooms.

And behind every shadow there is a light.

It might be a sun.

It might be a moon.

Behind our shadow is a light that I see inside of you.

On the last day, before you leave. We stay in bed.

We watched a science fiction movie, full of stars.

Afterwards I said that one day, I would like to walk in the moonlit forest under the stars with you and create our own interstellar.

I need to learn the language of love.

But I cannot find the words.

Every time I find some words, within each letter and between each word, I find a thousand questions. Questions that can only be answered with a thousand silences.

And yet my body and my soul know the meanings. And my voice knows when the silence does not need a word.

I find myself listening to the silent words, and letting my body and soul journey into the silences.

Love.

The huge world contained inside this one small word.

A world untouched.

A world around me, and waiting inside me.

Waiting under my skin.

Waiting all my life.

Waiting for you.

To create a dictionary of love, I need to be in heaven.

Right now, I am with you.

Whenever I am with you, I am in heaven.

X

DICTIONARY OF LOVE

Written for my lover.

I am feeling your body with my fingertips.
When I touch your body, I am touching
love.
I touch as if I am touching the maker of
the universe.
I touch the creator of life.
I touch the creator of love.
I touch the divine touch.

When my arms are around you.
I am holding you.
I am holding my world.
I am holding my heaven.

Every time I hold you it feels like the first

time.

Because before you, there was only a
hope, a wish, a dream.

When I am holding you,

I am worshipping love.

I am worshipping you.

Holding you brings me closer to god
than any religion, priest, prayer book,
temple or sermon.

I am holding the divine, the bliss, love,
in my arms.

I am feeling your body with my lips.
When I kiss your body, your skin, I am
kissing life.

The life I want to live.

The life I want to touch.

Each kiss is a prayer of gratitude that
you are in my world.

And when my lips sense the waking of
life under your skin,

I am kissing the creation of heaven.

When I see you enter the room and I am
the reason for your smile,
My heart leaps.
My soul lifts and flies to embrace you.

I feel a lightness in my body.
My body floats in your smile.
A wave of butterflies surprise me as
they fly through my body.
My soul worships your smile.
I am in awe, that the beauty and joy
inside you is loving me.

When my hand caresses your face, I am
touching the smile, the love.
The smile that takes me to another
world, another existence.
Another life.
I am no longer here.
I no longer exist.
Only my touch exists.
I am touching your face.
I am loving you.

When I kiss your lips,
I drown in the kiss.
The kiss takes me to another world,
another existence.
Another life.
I am no longer here.
I no longer exist.
Only the touch of my lips exists.

My kiss offers you every cell of love
inside me.

I stroke your hair.
When my fingers wander through your
hair,
I am remembering a moment.
I am making love with you.
My fingers touch the hair that carry the
memory of every moment of love we
have shared.
I want to feel the moments again with
you.

When I feel your waist,
I desire you.

When I feel your breast,
I want you to sense my desire.

When I am feeling your back,
I am making love with you.

When I look at your eyes,
Your eyes take me.
Your eyes fill me.

I am lost in a moment of ecstasy, a
moment of bliss.
I want to lay down with you.

When I feel your hand arrive in mine,
The missing part of me also arrives.
I am complete again.
My world is whole again.

When we are walking and I feel your hand
in mine,
I do not need to look at you.
Because I can feel you.
I cannot see your face.
And yet, I see your smile.
I see your eyes.
I feel your soul.
How is this possible?
I am touching the love inside you,
And your love is now inside me.
And my love is inside you.

When I watch you undress,
I am undressing you. I always want to
undress you.

When we are sitting together and I put my hand on your thigh,
I am remembering a kiss, a touch, a moment. I am feeling the moment again with you.

When I smell your clothes, smell your skin, smell your hair,
I smell our love.

When I wake and see you next to me,
There are no words.
Every sunset, I sleep knowing that I will wake with you.
And there are no words.
Only heaven.

XI

SILVER SCREEN

What happens next?

We go to a movie. We cuddle.
The scene is too real.
'How did you choose that movie?' you
laugh. A nervous laugh.
The scene continues. He asks her to
join him as he travels. She says she needs
to work. He tells her she can work
anywhere. She knows what he means.
You laugh again.
Afterwards you tell me you are heavy,
confused. Too much flowing through your
head.

But the sun is shining. The clouds are
soft today. The harshness of the rain has

been swept away by the winds of the night.

We talk about following your dreams.

I know I accept you, love you as you are. And that means accepting what you do, what you choose to do, where you are.

I cannot ask you to escape, or come away with me to my hidden sanctuaries in other lands. I have already woken to my selfishness. I know. I accept. And I will listen. Try and listen. The universe is constantly talking. Guiding.

Everything will be ok, I say to you. And I know it will be. A deeper knowing. A dream I once had.

And I know that if the root of love that we are experiencing is as special, as unique, and as rare as you say, as people say, then that magical tree that the root belongs to, that I have always believed in, the one under which Abraham once sheltered, will grow into something that will cover the entire world. Whichever world we happen to be in.

You tell me your fear. How long will our relationship last?

I say it does not matter.

I know I have already given myself to this moment.

And as much as I dream of loving and making love with you in every country from Indonesia to Iceland, I wake to the fragility of love. The fear of a hope that shatters. A wave from a dream that crashes on a shore. A heart that does not need, and choose not to need any more pain.

I do not want pain either, I think to myself. I only want to know love, give love, feel love, know your love, share love, make love.

I want you to smile forever.

Know yourself, be yourself. Be.

I want to walk into heaven with you.

I want to discover, be introduced to the god of love with you.

I want to feel the spirit of life with you.

I want to share the sunlight and sunrise and make love under the stars.

I want the shade of the tree to feel our love and bloom the flowers to feed nectar to the butterflies.

The butterflies that will surround us when we walk through the forest together.

The butterflies that recognise prayer and worship.

I have been praying all my life for love.

And now you are in my life.

I worship the creator of love through you.

What happens next? I do not know.

The next is only the now. And now is the rest of my life.

And there is only one word that matters more to me than anything else, more than life itself.

That word?

Between I and You?

Love.

XII

NO WORDS

The Man Who Fell In Love

Jon Persico

The Man Who Fell In Love

XIII

NO MORE

We are no longer.
No longer together.
It does not matter why.
Nothing to analyse.
Nothing to explain.
You accept.
I accept.

This morning, and in the mornings to come, when I wake, I turn around, I still look for you.
You have become a dream once more.
I do not remember my dreams.
But I remember our painting.
I remember the embrace.
I remember the softness of your neck on my lips, the shining of the dawnlight in

your hair, I still remember the joy I felt every morning when I opened my eyes.

I cannot hear you breathing, because you are no longer here.

But you are not a dream, you are not a painting.

You were real.

These are my new mornings.

Know that I loved you.

Know that my body was dead when you found me.

When we broke up, parted, my feelings overflowed.

For a while I felt that I died, a second time. A second death. I grieved.

My hearts stopped.

One heart looked for you and was torn when it did not find you.

One heart sobbed. At the most unexpected moments, the tears came.

One heart felt lost, even devastated.

What did the sense of loss and tears mean?

Heartbreak, oblivion, rejection, anger, self pity?

I found myself singing the pain.

And when I sang loudly, and when I realised the pain I felt was because I had loved, and felt so much of your love, I had no choice but to feel, embrace, accept and to even love the pain.

Because the pain was a testament, a witness, that I had loved. The pain was an acceptance of loss and that you were no longer there to accept my love.

The pain that my life would not know your love, your touch, your look, your eyes ever again.

I grieved the loss of no longer being able to love you. Hug you. Hold your hand in mine.

That raw feeling,

That simple feeling.

That feeling was no longer.

Yes, I wept.

I felt every metaphor.

Every synonym.

Every breath, every tear, every rip of the heart.

Because it was the first time I have felt a broken heart.

Imagine, the first time in my life I have felt a broken heart!

Through you, I felt love and loved like never before in my life.
I learned the meaning of the word.
A small word full of beautiful feelings.
A word that is very real, just like life.

Leaving love behind, I left a life behind.

Time does not heal.
Learning to watch love step further away.
Learning not to run after the love that is past.
To let go of your love was hard. If learning to accept love was difficult, to let go was harder.

Time does not heal.
Time changes.
Sad, heartbroken, but also feeling life for the first time.

For the first time in my life I feel alive like I have never felt before.

My soul, my body had never loved before you, I was empty before.

Yes, I sense the emptiness without you, there is sadness, heartbreak, of course. But this is a different, a new solitude.

Your love filled me, you accepting my love, completed me. The love you gave me is alive inside me. Every moment we shared, every touch and feeling of love that you gave me, is living inside me.

I walk a memory of smiles that I never had before.

I carry memories of feelings and sensations, and a knowing that I lived a life with you. And with you, I have been more loved, than I have ever been in my life.

I will never feel the same love again. Your love. I know.

And, right now, I feel a melancholy when I remember this knowing.

But I will always feel glad to know your love. To have known your love.

When I see two lovers look at each other's eyes in a restaurant, in the metro, in a bar, I remember our love.

Our lovemaking.

Our completeness.

And I wish it for them.

I wish for them to feel the warmth I felt with you.

To know that someone else has loved, is being loved as we loved each other, fills me with a knowing smile.

I smile with them. With their smile.

It is the same smile we had in the cafe when the waitress looked at us, and smiled at us. She knew something, saw something between us that we could not know, she could not know, only feel.

She felt the energy from the magical feelings between us.

I know I lived a love that I will never live again.

I fell into love.

I fell into you.

I fell in love.

And it was with you.

And for the first time in my life, I felt real.

Love.

XIV

TWO WORDS

Two words?
I almost forgot.
Two words to a lover.
Said with a genuine heart.
Two words that mean more than
anything else.
More than love.
More than life.
Two words before you close your eyes.

Thank you.

ABOUT THE AUTHOR

Jon Persico lives in Italy and India.

This is a first novel.